P9-DOA-926

Please Write in This Book

Please Write in This Book

by **Mary Amato**

illustrated by
Eric Brace

Holiday House / New York

Text copyright © 2006 by Mary Amato
Illustrations copyright © 2006 by Eric Brace
All Rights Reserved
Printed in the United States of America
www.holidayhouse.com
First Edition
1   3   5   7   9   10   8   6   4   2

Library of Congress Cataloging-in-Publication Data

Amato, Mary.
Please write in this book / by Mary Amato ;
illustrated by Eric Brace.—1st ed.
p.   cm.
Summary: When Ms. Wurtz leaves a blank book in the Writer's Corner
with a note encouraging those who find it to "talk to each other" in
its pages, the students' entries spark a classroom-wide battle.
ISBN-10: 0-8234-1932-0 hardcover
ISBN-13: 978-0-8234-1932-6 hardcover
[1. Authorship—Fiction. 2. Schools—Fiction.] I. Brace, Eric, ill. II. Title
PZ7.A49165Ple   2006
[Fic]—dc22   2005052678

For Simon, his friends from Highland
View Elementary School, and his
former teachers—especially Mindy
LeBlanc and Elisabeth Curtz
M. A.

For my niece and nephew, Clare and Eric,
who are okay at journaling,
but are even better pen pals
E. B.

Tuesday, August 31

Hello, Boys and Girls,

You have found this book! I hid it in the Writer's Corner, hoping you would.

During Center Time, you can choose to come to the Writer's Corner and write in this journal. Write about anything you want. Leave it for other students to find and write in, too. I want you to "talk" to one another in these pages.

I will read the book at the end of each month. But don't worry—I won't grade you on what you write.

There are only two rules:

1. Have fun.

2. Sign your name, so everyone knows who you are.

Your teacher,

Ms. Wurtz

P.S. Don't tell anybody else about this book. It will be more fun if each student finds it on his or her own.

Ms. Wurtz

Wednesday, September 1

Hi!

    My name is Lizzy. It is Center Time. During Center Time, you get to choose an activity at a center. There's Computer Center, Book Nook, Pet Center, Art Center, and Writer's Corner. I love writing, so I picked the Writer's Corner. I was going to write a beautiful poem on a piece of paper, but then I found this book telling me to please write in it. So now I'm the very first person to write in it. I love this idea. It is fun and educational. I can't wait to see who writes in it next. I hope only girls find it.

              Love,
              Lizzy

P.S. I'm not going to tell anybody else about this book.

Hello . . .

My name is Yoshiko. Lizzy told me to come to the Writer's Corner. She said it was a secret. She is my best friend. So I followed Lizzy here and found this book. Thank you, Ms. Wurtz!

Thursday, September 2

Howdy,
    My name is Luke. It rhymes with puke.

Luke,
    This is supposed to be a nice book. Nobody wants to see pictures of you barfing in it. —Lizzy

I agree with Lizzy. —Yoshi

Hey, Luke,

   Great picture. Made me laugh so hard, snot almost came out my nose.

                    Your pal,
                    Tyrone

Tyrone, Old Pal,
   Do you mean to say that muckus came out your honker? —Luke

Dear Class,

    This is Carmen. I am worried. Do you think this is really what Ms. Wurtz had in mind? Also, do you think it's okay to draw pictures? She didn't say we could draw pictures.

But here's a picture of me anyway.

New Rule by Lizzy: You may draw pictures, as long as they are nice!

Friday,
September 3

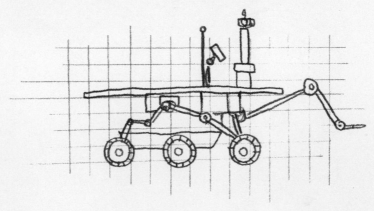

To: All
From: Milton

    I think that Ms. Wurtz wants us to write facts about things we're learning. Here is a fact: Today we learned that roving robots are invented for many purposes. My favorite robots are the ones used to explore other planets. Also, I think we should draw diagrams, such as this diagram of a roving robot that digs and collects rocks on Mars.

Dear Chums,

Although Milton's diagram is cool, it is a fact that facts are usually boring.

It is also a fact that Milton has a roving robot up his honker.

Yours truly,
Luke

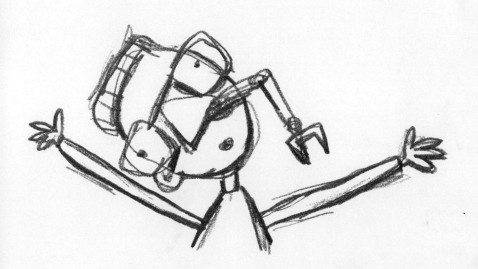

To: All

From: Milton

Luke is ridiculous. I could not have a roving robot up my nose. The one in my diagram would be over 3 feet long.

Milton, Old Chum,

That is big. You must not have any room in your honker for snot.

Your pal,
Luke

News Flash

by Tyrone

Luke is very funny. Also, we have an awesome new class pet. A hermit crab named Crazy.

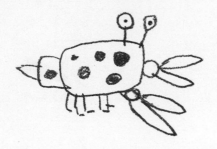

Hello, Everybody,
   Keesha here. I like this book! I didn't find it right away because I was in the Pet Center feeding the guppies.

Facts are not boring if they are about animals—especially horses. I wish we could have a horse for a class pet. But a crab is better than nothing.

P.S. I'm only good at drawing horses.

I ♡ HORSES

Monday, September 6

Dear Class,

    I think it's unfair that I didn't get the chance to write in this book on Friday. People shouldn't spend so much time drawing pictures of things going up other people's noses.

    I wanted to write the news about our new class pet. I wish Ms. Wurtz would have brought in something furry and cute for a pet, like a bunny. But here is a poem about Crazy the Crab.

        Love,

        Lizzy

Our New Class Pet

Why O Why
Are you so shy?
Come out of your shell!
We love you so well.
Even though you aren't cute
We'll never step on you with a boot.

We won't hurt you!

A message to Lizzy from Yoshi . . .
   I love your poem. And your picture. You
are sooo talented. You should be a poet or an
artist when you grow up.

P.S. I agree about the rabbit.

Thank you, Yoshi! But I decided I'm going to be a
famous ballet dancer. —Lizzy

Hermit Crab Fact by Milton

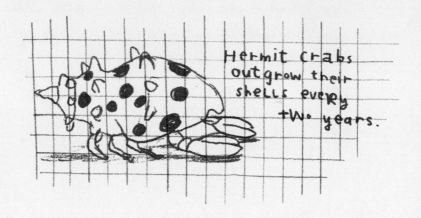

Hermit crabs outgrow their shells every two years.

Hey,

Do crabs have noses? If not, how does their snot come out?

—Tyrone

T-Bone,
    Good question. Why don't we put pepper in Crazy's cage and see if he sneezes?
                        Your pal,
                        Luke

Tuesday, September 7

A True Story About Crazy the Crab

by Luke

It is Center Time right now. Everybody is glaring at me because I got to the Writer's Corner first. Everybody wants to write in this book, except Jimmy. He hates to write.

Here's what happened today. My pal T-Bone and I went to the Pet Center first thing in the morning. We wanted to make Crazy sneeze to see if snot would come out. Ms. Wurtz wouldn't let us put pepper in the cage. But she did let us take Crazy out. Crazy likes to scoot around on the carpet. He likes the way the carpet feels on his bare claws.

Lizzy was there. "That looks fun," she said. She took off her shoes and did the crab walk on the carpet.

Crazy waved a claw in the air. "Whew!" Crazy said. "Lizzy's feet sure do stink!"

My eyes popped out. "That crazy crab can talk!" I exclaimed.

"I can smell too, man," Crazy added. "And it sure do smell bad. I'm outta here." He ran.

T-Bone and I ran after him. "Come back!"

Crazy is fast. He disappeared under Ms. Wurtz's desk.

Everybody was looking for him.

"All this crab hunting is making me hungry," Ms. Wurtz said. Her lunch bag was on the floor. She picked it up and took a big bite of her sandwich. She froze like a statue.

Crazy had crawled into her sandwich. Now he was sticking out of her mouth like a giant alien jawbreaker!

Spitoooooooey! Ms. Wurtz spit him out. He

flew across the room and landed in his cage with a thunk.

"Are you okay, Crazy?" I asked.

Crazy looked up. "Tell Lizzy to keep her shoes on. Man, that girl's feet stink worse than rhino gas!"

The End

Hey, Luke,

Great story. I laughed so hard I fell off my chair.

Your friend,

T-Bone

Ha ha ha
ha ha ha

HA!—Jimmy

← me, Jimmy

To: Luke
From: Milton

That was a funny story. But the fact is: Crazy does not have a nose.

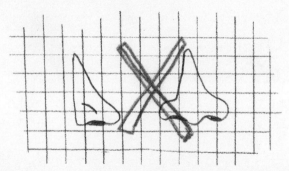

To Milton,

Wow. Crazy can smell Lizzy's feet, and he doesn't even have a nose! That means her feet must stink really bad. —Luke

HELP
ME!

Wednesday, September 8

Dear Class,

    Do <u>not</u> believe the story that Luke wrote yesterday. My feet do <u>not</u> stink. Crazy cannot talk. Crazy did <u>not</u> crawl into Ms. Wurtz's sandwich. It was all lies, lies, lies. And Luke is a Writer's Corner hog. He uses up all the Center Time so nobody else can write.

← Luke the hog

New Rules by Lizzy
1. You should not write mean things about other kids in this book.

2. You should not hog the Writer's Corner during Center Time.

A message to Luke from Yoshi . . .
   I agree with Lizzy. Please do not write any more mean things about my best friend in this book. Thank you.

To Yoshi:
   I wasn't being mean. I was being funny. Even Jimmy liked it. And Jimmy hates to read.
                        Yours truly,
                        Luke

To: All

From: Milton

Here's the problem. Can you prove that Luke was being funny? No. Can you prove that Luke was being mean? No. That's because whether or not Luke was being funny or mean is an *opinion*. That's why I like facts. Facts are things you can prove. Let's stick to the facts.

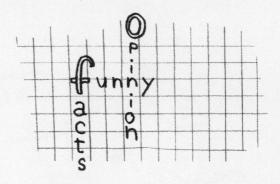

Luke,

If you weren't trying to be mean, then prove it. Write

something nice about me tomorrow to make up for it.

—Lizzy

Okey-dokey! From, Lukey Dukey

Thursday, September 9

Lizzy's Sweet-Smelling Feet

A Nice Story by Luke

During math today, Lizzy took off her shoes. Milton was sitting next to her. He had a roving robot up his honker. The robot flew out and explored Lizzy's feet with its smell detectors. It said in a robot voice: "The feet of this earthling smell like cherry cupcakes!"

 Lizzy grinned.
We all sniffed her feet.
"Like frosting!"
"Like honey!"
"Sweet!"

"This is all very fascinating, but please get back to work," Ms. Wurtz said.

Lizzy didn't listen. She danced around the room. The smell of her feet floated out the windows.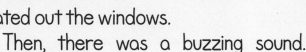

Then, there was a buzzing sound. *BZZZZzzzzzzz.*

Bees started flying in the windows. Lots of bees!

"Oh no!" Milton yelled. "It is a fact that bees love the smell of Lizzy's feet. Don't move, or they'll sting."

Lizzy stood still. So many bees landed on her feet, it looked like she was wearing fuzzy black-and-yellow slippers. "*Help!*" she yelled, and ran out of the room.

We followed. She ran up and down the halls, screaming, "Help! Help!" She ran into the lunchroom. "Help!"

27

"I'll help!" I said. I grabbed a trash can and dumped it on Lizzy.

Spaghetti and milk and tuna fish splattered all over her.

She smelled so horrible, the bees flew away.

"Thanks a lot, Luke," Lizzy said, picking noodles out of her hair.

"Any time," I said.

The End

HA, HA!—Jimmy

Hey, Luke,

I laughed so hard my teeth almost flew out. This is the funniest story in the whole world. When you grow up, you should be a book writer.

Your fan,
Tyrone

Keesha here. Speaking of horrible smells, some people think that horses smell bad. I love the way they smell. When I grow up, I want to be a horse.

← me as a horse

Speaking of horrible smells, take a whiff of Luke.
—Lizzy

I smell bad

Friday,
September 10

<u>Luke Puke</u>

Luke Puke has a problem.
He cannot tell the truth.
He is as bad
as a cavity in a tooth.

Luke Puke has
a problem.
He always tells
a lie.
I wish a witch
would turn him
into a big french fry.

News Flash

by T-Bone

Lizzy wrote a mean poem about Luke and didn't sign her name. She shouldn't make rules she can't keep. By the way, what if it's true that Lizzy's feet stink? Then wouldn't it be okay for Luke to write about them?

BOO LiZ!!

My Fellow Students,
T-Bone has an excellent point. Why don't we do an experiment? We could call it the Stinky Feet Experiment. We could all take off our shoes and see whose feet stink. It would be very scientific.
—Luke

Luke Puke,

Actually, I think maybe this experiment is a good idea. It will prove that my feet smell good, and then we can have a rule that nobody can say that they stink. I'll ask Ms. Wurtz if we can do it on Monday.

—Lizzy

 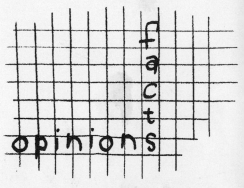

I agree with Lizzy. —Yoshi

To: All
From: Milton

No! Don't ask Ms. Wurtz to conduct this "experiment." It won't be scientific at all. Luke will think that Lizzy's feet smell bad, and Lizzy will think her feet  smell good. These are not facts that can be proven scientifically. They are opinions!

Dear Milty, Old Chap,
    Go with the flow! Have some fun for once in your life! Take off your shoes and get stinky!
        —Luke

Yeah. Get stinky. —Jimmy

Dear Class,
    This is Carmen. Today Ms. Wurtz said that she is glad that so many people want to go to the Writer's Corner. I don't think she realizes that people are writing about puke and stinky feet in here. I am

worried about this. What if Ms. Wurtz gets mad? Isn't anybody else worried about this?

Nope. –Luke

Nope. —T-Bone

Nope. –Jimmy

Not really. –Keesha

I don't think Ms. Wurtz will blame me for anything. Luke is the problem. –Lizzy

Luke the Puke

←

I just wish everybody would be nice to everybody all the time. —Yoshi

Don't worry, Carmen. Ms. Wurtz will not get mad at you. When she finds out what has been written, she'll probably require us to write only facts in here from now on. And that will solve the problem. —Milton

Monday, September 13

The Official Results of
the Stinky Feet Experiment

by Luke

Today our class did the Stinky Feet Experiment. We sat in a circle and took off our shoes. I

was sitting next to Ms. Wurtz. She sniffed my feet.

"No offense, Luke," Ms. Wurtz said. "But your feet smell like worms."

Tyrone was sitting next to me. I sniffed Tyrone's feet. "Well, T-Bone's feet smell like moldy muckus."

Tyrone sniffed Keesha's feet. "Well, Keesha's feet smell like horse poop."

Keesha sniffed Jimmy's feet. "Well, Jimmy's feet smell like fried seaweed."

Jimmy sniffed Milton's feet. "Well, Milton's feet smell like turkey vomit."

From his cage, Crazy the Crab begged: "Put your shoes back on or I'll . . ."

The poor crab fainted.

"Oh dear," Ms. Wurtz said. "Do you think we should go on?"

"We must go on," I replied. "In the name of science."

Milton sniffed Carmen's feet. "Well, Carmen's feet smell like dead mice."

Carmen sniffed Yoshiko's feet. "Well, I am worried about Yoshi's feet. They smell like cave mud."

Yoshi sniffed Lizzy's feet. "Well, Lizzy's feet smell like hairy mushrooms."

Ms. Wurtz was sitting next to Lizzy. "Do you really want me to smell your feet?" Lizzy asked Ms. Wurtz.

"Sure," Ms. Wurtz said. "I'm part of this activity."

Nervously, Lizzy sniffed Ms. Wurtz's feet.

"It's okay to tell the truth, Lizzy," Ms. Wurtz said.

"Well, your feet smell like a garbage can full of old pig guts that's been sitting in the sun too long."

Ms. Wurtz picked Lizzy up and threw her out the window.

Conclusion: Everybody's feet stink.

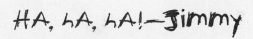

HA, hA, hA!—Jimmy

Tuesday,
September 14

Dear Class:

    I did <u>not</u> say that Ms. Wurtz's feet smell like old pig guts. I said that her feet smell like whole peanuts. I think peanuts smell go<u>od</u>. And Yoshi did not say my feet smell like hairy mushrooms. She said my feet smell like cherry blossoms. And the crab did <u>not</u> talk. And Ms. Wurtz did not throw me out the window.

    New Rule: If Luke does not improve, he will not be allowed to write in this book.

                    —Lizzy

To: All
From: Milton

I feel a need to set the record straight. Here is what happened yesterday morning.

Ms. Wurtz said: "Since so many of you are focused on foot odor, let's do the Stinky Feet Experiment. Everybody, take off your shoes and sit in a circle on the floor."

"But this isn't science!" I said. "It's based on opinion, not fact."

"Of course you're right, Milton," Ms. Wurtz said. "Don't think of it as a science experiment. Think of it as a language arts game. Here's what we'll do. Each of us will smell the feet of the next person over and come up with a *simile* to describe the odor. Do any of you know what a *simile* is?"

Lizzy raised her hand.

"Yes, Lizzy?"

"*Simile* is a poetic term. It means to describe something by saying it is like something else. For example: 'A cloud is like a soft pillow.' That is a simile."

"Right," Ms. Wurtz said. "Now, boys and girls, if you want to play this game, you have to agree to be a good sport. If Lizzy says your

40

feet smell like rotten bananas, laugh about it. No getting sad or mad. It's just a fun exercise."

So we sat in a circle and played the game. It didn't prove anything, but it was a way to practice similes.

By the way, I didn't say Carmen's feet smell like dead mice. I said they smell like detritus. Detritus is the muck you find in swamps that smells like rotten eggs. Note to Luke: There is no such word as *muckus*. When you said that Tyrone's feet smell like moldy muckus, I think you meant *mucus*.

rotten eggs

Dear Milton, Old Buddy,
    I like muckus better. It's more mucky.
                    Your pal,
                    Luke

P.S. Hey, Lizzy, here's my New Rule: No one is allowed to make up new rules.

NO NEW RULES

Keesha here. Tyrone did say that my feet smell like horse poop. But I don't mind. I can't wait until tomorrow. Since September is Getting-to-Know-You Month, Ms. Wurtz is letting us each bring in something we collect to share with the class. I am bringing in my entire horse collection. I have a feeling it's going to be the best day of my life.

Wednesd—
Wednesday,
September 15

Keesha here. Today, I brought my horse collection in a box. It didn't fit in my cubby, so I had to put it by the door.

We had math first.

"Keesha! Stop wiggling your feet," Ms. Wurtz said.

"Keesha can't wait to show her collection," Jimmy said.

Jimmy was right. It is very hard to go like this:

$$345 \times 3 = \underline{\hspace{2cm}}$$

when 167 horses are by the door.

Ms. Wurtz said: "Well, perhaps we should let Keesha share her collection now and do math later."

Everybody cheered. Except Carmen. She was worried about not doing math.

I pulled the first horse out. "This is Black Beauty."

I pulled the second horse out. "This is Big Red."

I pulled the third horse out—

"Is she going to show them all?" Carmen asked. She was still worried about not doing math.

"I've got to show them all!" I said. "Or it won't be right."

"Oh dear," said Ms. Wurtz.

I got a bad feeling in my stomach, like this wasn't going to be the best day of my life.

"Let's use Keesha's horse collection to practice some of our math concepts," Ms. Wurtz said. "Can you estimate how long the line would be if we lined up all Keesha's horses?"

We *estimated* the *length*. Then we made a line of all my horses that went out the door! Then we *measured* it in feet and meters. We also found the *average* size of the horses.

I love Ms. Wurtz. Almost as much as horses.

The End

News Flash

by Tyrone

Today, something funny happened. Turn back two pages before this one and look at the date. You know why it's scribbly at the top? I'm going to explain because it's a good story. When Ms. Wurtz said it was Center Time, Keesha started walking to the Writer's Corner. Then Luke and Lizzy both ran for it. Luke got there first, of course. Fair and square. But Lizzy pushed him off the chair and sat down. She started writing the date, so Luke got up and grabbed the pen right out of her hand.

"Give it back," she yelled.

"I was there first," he yelled.

"Both of you go back to your desks!" Ms. Wurtz said. "I want you to be excited about writing, but I don't want you to fight about it. It is a Writer's Corner, not a Boxing Corner."

"Hey," Jimmy said. "That gives me a good idea. Let's have a Boxing Corner!" He jumped up and started boxing me. So I boxed back.

"For heaven's sake," Ms. Wurtz said. "Everybody has a lot of energy today. I think we need to get it all out. For the next sixty seconds, we are going to have Air Boxing. Everyone stand up."

"Are you sure this is okay?" Carmen asked.

"There should be a rule about no hurting," Lizzy said.

"We aren't boxing each other. We are boxing the air," Ms. Wurtz said. "And you must stop when I say the time is up. Ready?"

Everybody jumped up and started boxing the air. Even Ms. Wurtz. *Pow! Pow!*

"Look at my fancy footwork," Ms. Wurtz said. We all laughed because she looked like a crazy kangaroo. *Pow! Pow!*

Thursday, September 16

Hello, Class,

This is Lizzy. I got to the Writer's Corner first today. Fair and square. Ha, ha, Luke. I am going to do us all a big favor and write about something nice. This morning, it was my day to share something from home. I brought in my collection of ballet costumes called <u>tutus</u>. Ms. Wurtz let me put on the beautiful pink tutu and do a demonstration. Here is a poem about it. It has a *simile* in it.

<u>Sugar Plum Fairy</u>

by Lizzy

I danced like a fairy floating on the air.
I felt like I had wings on and sparkles in my hair.

Every step was perfect. I twirled without fear.

When I ended with a bow, everyone did cheer. Then I slipped on a dead mouse and fell on my pink rear.

This is Lizzy again. I am really mad. I did <u>NOT</u> write that part about slipping and I did <u>NOT</u> draw that picture at the end. <u>Luke</u> did it.

There needs to be a New Rule: <u>No Writing or Drawing on Anybody Else's Stuff.</u> And Luke needs to apologize. Or else.

—Lizzy

Dear Lizzy,

I'm sorry for saying that you fell on your pink rear. I shouldn't have written that. I don't know what color your rear is.

–Luke

HA, hA, hA, hA, hA!—Jimmy

Keesha here. My mom says it's more proper to say "buttocks." By the way, the rear ends of horses are often called "rumps."

Rump →

Friday, September 17

Dear Class,
    This is Carmen. I am very worried. Now people are writing about rear ends. What if Ms. Wurtz yells at us and shows this book to the principal? Maybe we should rip out the pages and start again?

← **Mad Principal Stevens**

Dear Carmen:
    Rip out the pages? Are you insane? Did you fall on your buttocks and damage your brain? This book is a masterpiece. T-Bone and Jimmy agree.

          –Luke

MaSterpiece →

A message to Luke from Yoshi...

I think the problem is that you're not following Lizzy's rules. They are very good rules. I went back and found them all. Here they are:

1. You may draw pictures, as long as they are nice.
2. You should not write mean things about other kids in this book.
3. You should not hog the Writer's Corner during Center Time.
4. If Luke does not improve, he will not be allowed to write in this book.
5. No writing or drawing on anybody else's stuff.

Here are some drawings of nice things.

News Flash

by T-Bone

Lizzy is not the Boss of the Universe or the Queen Rule Maker. Besides, Lizzy has written mean things about Luke in here. I like Luke's rule: No New Rules.

To: All
From: Milton
The fact is Ms. Wurtz gave us only two rules:
1) Have fun.
2) Sign your name.
She probably should have written the rule: Stick to the facts. But she didn't.

Another message to Luke from Yoshi . . .
Well, it seems like you're picking on my best friend Lizzy. Please leave her alone and write a funny story about somebody else. Thank you.

Yo, Yoshi,
Great idea. Next time I will.
Yours truly,
Lukey Boy

Monday, September 20

Worm Day

by Luke

Today was a thrilling day for students in Ms. Wurtz's class. I brought in my collection to share. When all the students were sitting on their buttocks at their desks, I said: "Close your eyes and open your hands." Then I put worms in their hands. I have a very large worm collection.

"Open your eyes," I said.

Everybody fainted. When they woke up, I shared worm facts with the class. Like the fact that worms eat dirt and poop all over the place even though they don't have buttocks. And the

fact that worms really
like me.

NO buttocks

Then it was time
for art.

"Luke, put your worms back in your can and
line up for art, please," Ms. Wurtz said.

The worms looked at me. The leader of the
worms said: "Please let us come with you, sir!"

I put them all on the ground and they wriggled after me like a little fan club. "We will follow
you anywhere, sir!" they said.

In art, the worms helped me
paint. They make great
paintbrushes.

Then I went to
computer lab. The worms
helped me type by jumping on the keys.

Then it was time for lunch.

"The worms cannot follow you to lunch,"
Yoshi said. "That would be against the rules."

"You're right," I said. I turned to face my
little fan club. "Worms! Please follow her to
lunch." I pointed at Yoshi.

"Yes, sir!" the worms said, and mobbed her.

Yoshi screamed, jumped out the window, and landed on her rump.

The End

To: All

From: Milton

Although Luke's story is clearly fictional, he did state several facts about worms. They don't have buttocks. The front end is called the anterior and the rear end is called the posterior. Their waste makes excellent fertilizer. Here is a diagram of a worm. Note that they do not have eyes. Worms are blind.

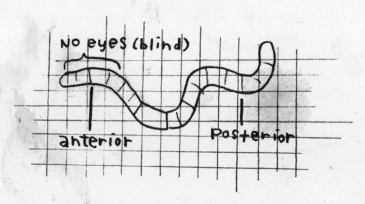

NO eyes (blind)

anterior

Posterior

News Flash

by T-Bone

Luke's worms rule.

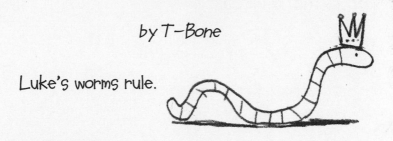

BuTTOCKS! HA, hA, hA, hA, hA, hA!—Jimmy

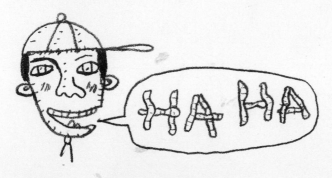

Luke (and Tyrone and Jimmy),
   That was <u>not</u> funny. Tomorrow, I will show
                    you something funny.
                              —Lizzy

Dear Lizzy,
   Is that a threat?

                    Yours truly,
                    Luke

                              O

Dear Luke,
   Yes. I hope you're scared.

                    Yours truly (and cruelly),
                    Lizzy

Tuesday, September 21

Worm Day, Part II

by Luke

Well, I guess I got to the Writer's Corner first. Fair and square. Sorry, Lizzy. But have I got a story to tell.

Remember my worms? Well, I left them in my cubby overnight, and this morning, they read Lizzy's threat in this book. (My worms happen to be excellent readers.) As you can imagine, her threat made them mad.

"Sir," the leader of the worms said. "Let us teach Lizzy and her friend Yoshi a lesson."

"Okey-dokey," I replied.

So the worms all crawled out of their can.

"We are going to pounce on Lizzy and Yoshi," the leader said. "But we need more worms. Send the signal."

The worms pounded their posteriors on the ground, sending a signal through the concrete floor of the school, all the way into the ground.

Millions and millions of worms crawled up out of their tunnels. They wriggled in through the school windows and gathered together.

Lizzy and Yoshi did not notice because they were busy whispering to each other.

"Let's pounce!" yelled the worm leader, pointing at Lizzy and Yoshi. Off they went. Let me tell you, when my worms want to, they can crawl really fast.

"Aaaah!" Lizzy and Yoshi screamed and ran up the stairs to the library.

The worms followed them in. I followed, too. I did not want to miss this.

"We're being chased by worms!" Lizzy said.

"Shhh," the librarian said.

Lizzy tried to explain. "But—but—"

"*Shhh*," the librarian said. "Especially no talking about rear ends!"

The leader faced his worms. "Sock Shock! Now!" he yelled. A bunch of worms pounced on the girls' feet and pulled down their socks.

"*Aaaaah!*" they screamed.

"Girls, stop that yelling," said the librarian. "If you're not checking out a book, please leave."

"Mustache Mob! Now!" called the leader. Two very strong worms jumped and landed like mustaches under the honkers of Lizzy and Yoshi.

"*Yuck!*" the girls screamed.

The worms didn't stop. "Hair Heap! Now!" the leader yelled. The worms leaped into heaps on Lizzy's and Yoshi's hair.

The girls screamed and ran around. "Help! We're sorry!"

"Stop, worms!" I shouted.

The worms jumped down and landed on their posteriors, and the room grew quiet.

"Luke, thank you for stopping all that commotion," the librarian said. "Those two girls are very noisy."

The End

News Flash

by T-Bone

Luke writes a masterpiece!

MUSTACHE MOB! HA!

—Jimmy

Wednesday,
September 22

The Three
Meanies

A True Poem

by Lizzy

Our class has three fools.
They think they're really cool.
They're really, really not.
Their brains are filled with snot.
Their names are Luke, Tyrone, and Jimmy.
They always shake and shimmy.
They're called The Three Meanies,
And they love to wear bikinis!

Thursday,
September 23

CRABBY Lizzy

A True Poem

By Jimmy

Lizzy is a CRAB
And a BOSS And a Liar.
We've Locked her in a Cage.
Do you want to Buy her?

Jimmy, Old Chum,
    Wow!!! I give your poem a gold star and an A+! Here's a picture to go with it.
                              Your pal,
                              Luke

News Flash

by T-Bone

Jimmy is a poet, and we didn't even know it.

Friday, September 24

<u>New Rule: This book is the private property of Lizzy and Yoshiko</u>

This is Lizzy. I am writing this in the girl's bathroom! Yoshi is here, too. We are hiding this book because Luke and Tyrone and Jimmy will just keep writing lies and mean stuff. We're going to come to the bathroom every day during Center Time and write in this book.

Dear Lizzy,
    Aren't we going to tell Carmen and Keesha? And what about Milton? He didn't write anything mean.

                    Love,
                    Yoshi

Dear Yoshi,
    Let's not tell them. Carmen will just worry. Milton will just want to write facts. And Keesha will just want to write about horses. Let's just have it be you and me. Don't tell anybody where we're hiding it. Let's meet back here after recess.
                    Love,
                    Lizzy

        me + you = Recess
                   ToGetHer

News Flash

by T-Bone

Stolen book is found!

Guess where Luke and Jimmy and I are? We're in the boys' bathroom! We rescued this book from the Chief Thief, otherwise known as Lizzy the Lizard. Luke and I both wanted to write down the story of how we got it back, so we flipped a coin. I won.

Here's the whole story. During Center Time this morning, nobody could find this book. Everybody was really upset. Except Lizzy. She tried to look upset, but her eyeballs looked excited. Then she and Yoshi spent a lot of time in the bathroom.

On the playground during recess, Luke said: "I think they hid the book in the girls' bathroom. Let's go check it out."

"But we're not allowed in until the bell rings," Jimmy said.

"He's right," I said. "We need a plan."

Luke snapped his fingers. "What if I fell and got hurt and I couldn't walk very good and I needed you guys to help me into the bathroom to wash it off?"

"That's a great idea!" I said. "Then we could sneak into the girls' bathroom."

"But you're not hurt," Jimmy said.

Luke fell down and grabbed his knee. "Ouch! Ouch! My knee!"

With our help, he limped over to the recess teacher. She let us in!

The hallways were empty. Quietly, we sneaked past the boys' bathroom to the door marked Girls. We opened the door a crack and listened. No sounds were coming from inside. We crept in like spies . . . and came face-to-face with two little kindergarteners.

"*Boys!*" the girls screamed, and ran out.

We found the book hidden on top of the paper towel box. Luke is going to hide it in his backpack.

We're going to show it secretly to everybody but Lizzy and Yoshi. Everybody is going to be mad at them.

Gotta go. Recess is almost over. When Lizzy and Yoshi go into the girls' bathroom, they'll find out that the book is gone. They'll be upset. They'll think the janitor threw it away or turned it in to the principal or something. And the rest of us are going to pretend like nothing is going on.

Monday, during Center Time, we're going to put it back in the Writer's Corner. Lizzy and Yoshi will have heart attacks. It will be so funny.

Monday,
September 27

Dear Lizzy and Yoshi,

   As you can see, your little plan to hide the book failed. We found it on Friday! We all read it and voted to give you new nicknames: The Queens of Mean.

                                   —Your Fellow Students

This is Carmen. Tyrone said it was going to be funny when Lizzy and Yoshi found the book and read the letter. It wasn't funny. Yoshi burst into tears and ran into the girls' bathroom.

She is still in there crying, and she says she won't come out. She says she's sorry. She doesn't think anybody will forgive her or Lizzy. She says everybody hates them.

I think it was wrong of them to hide the book, but I don't hate them. I feel bad that Yoshi is crying. And I am worried that she won't stop.

Ms. Wurtz is worried, too. She knows that this book is causing a problem. She said we have to work together to solve the problem or else she'll have to take the book away.

What are we going to do?

Keesha here. I am going to tell Yoshi my secret formula for cheering up. Here it is. Close your eyes and imagine you're riding through a field of flowers on a big horse named Gumball. That always works for me.

I KNOW A WAY to GET YoShi to COME OUT OF the BAthROOM! T-BonE AnD LuKE AnD I COULD SNEAK IN AnD StICK LotS OF toiLEt pApER in the toiLEtS to MAKE them OVERFLOW. ThAt WOULD MAKE YoShi COME OUT!
—Jimmy

That is <u>not</u> funny—Lizzy

I KNOW. I WROTE it BECAUSE I feel BAD ABOUT YoShi, AND I DIDN'T KNOW WHAT else to write. —Jimmy

News Flash

by Tyrone

I am sorry that we made Yoshi cry. But I think Lizzy should say she's sorry, too. It was her idea to steal this book.

sorry!

Dear Class,

It was my idea. I'm sorry that I hid the book from you. But I was mad at Luke and Jimmy and Tyrone for ganging up on me and Yoshi.

And I'm really sorry that I wrote that stuff about not wanting Milton or Keesha or Carmen to write in it. I take it back. I'm sorry, sorry, sorry. You can write whatever you want. Please don't be mad at me or Yoshi.

If Luke promises not to write any more lies or mean stuff about me and Yoshi, I promise not to write any more lies or mean stuff about him and Jimmy and Tyrone.

Love,
Lizzy

Me and Yoshi, almost dead.

P.S. I'm still kind of mad at Luke for not telling us right away that they found the book. And for making the rest of the class go along with the plan. Yoshi and I felt so bad all weekend, we almost died because we thought the book was lost.

Okay. Okay.

I guess it was mean to keep the book all weekend. And I guess I did get carried away with some of my stories (even if they were funny). I'm sorry.

But enough of this gushy stuff.

We need a plan.

What if we all agree to write one big story? If we all agree to write fiction, then we'll all know

that the story isn't real. It's like what Ms. Wurtz said about the stinky feet. Make stuff up and be a good sport. No getting sad or mad. It's just fun.
—Luke

Dear Luke,

Actually, I think that's not a bad idea. We can try it as long as everybody promises not to pick on me or Yoshi. —Lizzy

Dear Lizzy,
    <u>And</u> as long as you promise not to be so bossy.
                    —Luke

To: All
From: Milton
    I don't really know how to write a make-believe story.

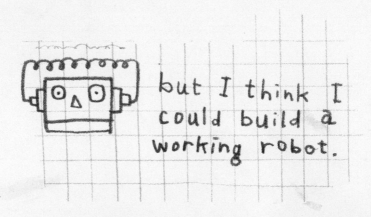

but I think I could build a working robot.

Dear Milton,

    Here's my secret formula for writing a great story. Start with the facts. Describe something that really happened—like you came to school—but then ask yourself *what if* something unexpected happened next—like the guppies in the Pet Center hopped out of the tank and jumped down your pants? Make stuff up.

Your pal,
Luke

To: Luke

From: Milton

    I like your secret formula. But should we label the story FICTION? That way anyone else who reads this book will know that it isn't really true. Otherwise, there could be some confusion. For example, what if a spacecraft from another planet took our journal as a part of their mission to find out about our planet? Without a label, the aliens would think the story was true.

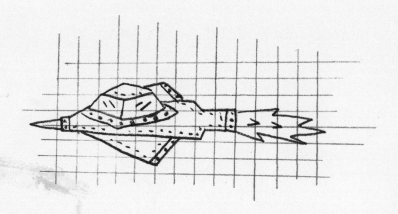

Milton, Old Chap,
    What if aliens steal our book? What a great story idea! Okay, listen up, everybody. Tomorrow, Milton will start our story. He gets to write whatever he wants. Then everybody can take turns adding to the story. Now, Milton, go stick your head in the bathroom and tell Yoshi to come out because we have a plan.

Why me?

Because whenever a boy sticks his head in the girls' bathroom, girls scream. It's very funny.

Oh. I get it.

Tuesday,
September 28

A message to everyone from Yoshi . . .

Thank you for cheering me up. I am so sorry about hiding this journal.

I read everything you guys wrote. I like the idea of one big story. You guys are the best friends, and this is the best class in the whole world.

Dear Chummy Chums,

Okay. Okay. Like I said, enough of this gushy stuff. Ms. Wurtz is going to read this book at the end of the month. That's in two days! Let's get writing.

Milton, take it away. When you run out of ideas, hand the book to someone else.

—Luke

The Invasion of the Journal Snatchers

by Ms. Wurtz's Class

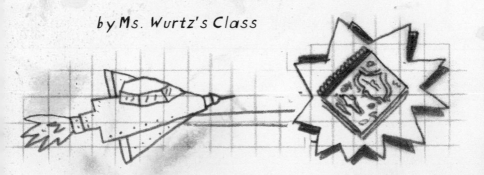

The day began in an ordinary way. It was a nice day, partly cloudy, temperature: 73°F.

When the school bell rang, we walked into Ms. Wurtz's room and sat down at our desks.

"Good morning," Ms. Wurtz said. "We are going to begin today with a spelling test. Please get out your pencils." She sat down. Only, her chair wasn't there. So she landed on her posterior.

"Ouch!" she said.

"Is that the first spelling word?" Luke asked.

Before Ms. Wurtz could answer, she was interrupted by a loud humming sound in the courtyard outside the window. The courtyard filled with a strange green light.

"That sunlight is unusual," Milton said. "Perhaps we should investigate—"

Before he could finish his sentence, the strange green light came in through the classroom windows. And when the light touched the skin of Ms. Wurtz and us, we all froze like statues.

We didn't know it, but it was no ordinary light. It was a Bio-Freeze Blaster Beam coming

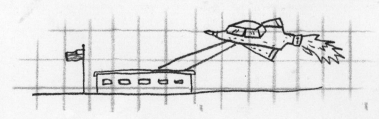

from an alien spacecraft that was hovering over the school.

We were frozen, so we didn't know what was happening . . . or how much time was passing.

When we woke up, the classroom looked exactly the same. Except two things were missing. Our book . . . and our teacher!

"What happened?"

"Where is Ms. Wurtz?"

"Where is our journal?"

We were all worried. Except Carmen, who was really worried.

How would we ever find out what happened?

A voice in the back of the room cried: "I know what happened!"

Everybody turned around. It was Crazy the Crab. "You turned into statues when that light touched your skin. But I hid in my shell, so I didn't get frozen. I heard everything. Two aliens came and took Ms. Wurtz and your book."

"What did they look like?" Yoshi asked.

"Did they look like horses?" Keesha asked.

"Tell us the facts!" Milton said.

"They were short and purple with curly toes and they wore pink hats that looked like tutus on their heads."

"They sound like Chummies from the Planet Chum," Milton said.

"We must save our teacher and our book from the Chummies," Lizzy said. "Let's all work together!"

So, we built an awesome rocket to take us to Planet Chum.

Everybody wanted to go. Even Luke's can of worms. Even Crazy the Crab.

5, 4, 3, 2, 1! Pow! We blasted off the earth and into outer space.

Boom! We landed on a pile of rocks. Fortunately, the pile of rocks was on Planet Chum. We got out.

"I'm worried," Carmen said. "There's nobody here."

"Look," Luke said. He pointed to a sign:

SCHOOL FOR THE STUDY OF CAPTURED EARTHLINGS

1,000 MILES THIS WAY

"I bet they are studying Ms. Wurtz," Tyrone said. "And reading our book! We've got to go there right now. But how?"

"Too bad I don't have a roving robot up my honker," Milton said. "That would've come in handy."

Keesha said, "Too bad we don't have horses to ride."

Suddenly, we heard a familiar humming sound.

"Here come the Chums," Crazy said.

A Chum spacecraft was headed our way!

Wednesday,
September 29

THE INVASION OF THE JOURNAL SNATCHERS (CONTINUED)

The chummies captured us and brought us to the School for the Study of Captured Earthlings.

"We do not want to hurt you," the Captain said. "We want to study you. We want to learn what it means to be human."

"What if we don't want to be studied?" Tyrone asked.

"Tough toenails," the captain growled.

"Well, that isn't very chummy," Luke said.

They marched us into a classroom. A group of chummy children were sitting around one table. They were reading our book. Another group of chummies were sitting around another table. They were studying Ms. Wurtz.

"Hello," Ms. Wurtz said to us. "You're late. Class has already begun."

Some of the children were smelling her feet. Others were looking up her nose.

"For some reason, they are very interested in feet and noses," Ms. Wurtz said.

The captain made us take off our shoes, and the chummies started sniffing our feet.

They even tried smelling Crazy's feet. "I ain't got no feet, you chumps!" Crazy yelled.

"We've got to get rid of them so we can escape," Luke whispered to us.

We all nodded.

"Chummy chums," Luke said. "There is only one way to learn what it means to be human. If you promise never to bother us again, we'll teach you the secret."

"Okey-dokey," the captain said.

The chummies all leaned forward, eager to hear the secret ...

Lizzy jumped in. She had a great idea. "First, get everybody together and go stand on that mountaintop over there." She pointed out the window at a faraway Chum mountain.
"And then dance the night away!"

"Everybody has to join in," Yoshi added.

"Yeah," Jimmy said. "Shake and shimmy."

"Get down!" said Crazy.

"Like this?" the captain asked. He wiggled his posterior, and it looked so fun and funny, all the other Chums started laughing.

"That's it! Now get everybody together and go over to that mountain," Milton said.

As soon as all the Chums were out of sight, we crept out.

There was a Chum spacecraft parked outside the school.

"I don't think they'd mind if we borrowed this, do you?" Ms. Wurtz asked.

We hopped in. We were doing it! We were finally escaping from Planet Chum.

As we blasted off, we looked out the spacecraft window. To the west, we could see the mountaintop. Chums of all shapes and sizes were dancing and laughing together.

It was a beautiful, happy sight!

"I think we have taught the Chums something about being human after all," Lizzy said with a smile and a sigh.

"Enough of this gushy stuff," Luke said. "Let's get back to Earth."

We blasted past the moon.

Pretty soon, we could see the United States of America below.

"Hey, Ms. Wurtz, since we rescued you, don't you think we deserve a treat?" Luke asked. "Instead of going back to school, let's go to the beach."

"We can go surfboarding!"

"Okey-dokey," Ms. Wurtz said.

So as the spacecraft flew over California, we jumped out.

"Aaaaahhhhh."

Fortunately, we remembered our parachutes.

"Wheeeeeee."

Unfortunately, the wind blew us away from the beach and into the desert.

"Nooooooooo."

As we floated nearer to the ground, Carmen asked: "What are all those green things below us?"

"Those are cactuses," Luke said. "We're about to land on cactuses!"

"Yiiiiiiiiiiiiiikes."

"Actually, the plural of *cactus* is *cacti*," Milton said. "We're about to land on cacti."

Cactuses. Cacti. Either way, it was going to be a pain.

As we came closer, we could see the nasty pricklers.

Ms. Wurtz said: "Can anyone think of a *simile* to describe how these prickles will feel?"

"Like a bed of rusty nails," Milton said.

"Like pointy killer-shark teeth," Jimmy said.

"Like hundreds of sharp, stinging splinters," suggested T-Bone.

"Ha, ha, suckers!" Crazy the Crab said. "You guys are going to get your posteriors pierced. I'm the only one who ain't scared. I got built-in body armor." He ducked inside his shell.

The cacti were getting closer and closer. We wished we had remembered to put our shoes on before we left Planet Chum.

"Ms. Wurtz," Milton asked, "aren't these the type of cacti that have poison in their spines?"

"Milton, I believe you're right," Ms. Wurtz said.

"*Heeeeeeeelp!*" we all screamed.

Keesha stuck two fingers in her mouth and whistled. She is really good at whistling. She whistled long and loud.

"No offense, Keesha," Ms. Wurtz said. "But I don't think a song will help us now."

"This isn't a song. It's a wild-horse call," Keesha explained. She whistled again. In the distance, we heard another sound. *Ba-da-dum! Ba-da-dum! Ba-da-dum! Ba-da-dum!*

It was the sound of thundering hoofbeats.

Ba-da-dum! Ba-da-dum! Ba-da-dum! Ba-da-dum!

Wild horses appeared!

"Noble horses have come to save us," Keesha said. "I get the biggest one!"

We landed on their backs.

"Thank you, noble horses, for answering my call," Keesha said.

"*Keeeeeeesha, Keeeeeeeesha,*" the horses whinnied.

As the sun set, we rode off across the desert,

through fields of flowers, and all the way to back to school.

When we got back to our classroom, Ms. Wurtz gave us cookies and juice.

"I can't believe how smart and brave you all are," Ms. Wurtz said. "You saved me! Tell the truth, now, weren't you just a little bit scared?"

"I wasn't worried," Carmen said. "I just looked worried."

The End

Thursday, September 30

Dear Boys and Girls,

    I can't believe you filled up this whole book in one month. I'm so glad you figured out how to work together.

                Your teacher,

                Ms. Wurtz

                P.S. Your story made me laugh so hard snot almost came out of my nose.

                P.P.S. Since you're out of pages, I'll have to get you a new book.

Gold Stars for everyone